Writings of a Random Bachelor

Marcel T. Despabeladero

Ukiyoto Publishing

All global publishing rights are held by

Ukiyoto Publishing

Published in 2025

Content Copyright © Marcel T. Despabeladero

ISBN 9789370097957

All rights reserved.

No part of this publication may be reproduced, transmitted, or stored in a retrieval system, in any form by any means, electronic, mechanical, photocopying, recording or otherwise, without the prior permission of the publisher.

The moral rights of the author have been asserted.

This book is sold subject to the condition that it shall not by way of trade or otherwise, be lent, resold, hired out or otherwise circulated, without the publisher's prior consent, in any form of binding or cover other than that in which it is published.

www.ukiyoto.com

Dedication

First and foremost, I thank God—for the gift of words, the strength to carry on, and the grace that has guided me through every chapter of my life.

To my mother, my fiercest supporter and my greatest blessing—thank you for raising me with love, strength, and unwavering belief in my dreams. This book would not exist without your sacrifices and encouragement.

To Taylor Swift—your music, your lyrics, and your fearless storytelling lit a spark in me. You showed me that vulnerability is a kind of power, and that heartbreak can be turned into art.

And to all the souls I've loved—thank you. Whether you stayed or left, whether it ended in silence or song, you've left echoes in my heart and ink on these pages. This book is as much yours as it is mine.

With all my heart,
Marcel.

Contents

Folklore	1
My Jennie	2
You Were	4
The Standard	5
One Last Time	7
Behold Her I	8
Behold Her II	9
Your Eyes	10
The Sweetest Con	12
Who Would Have Thought?	13
Serendipity	14
I Miss You	15
Questions	16
Enslaved	17
With You	19
Superman	20
Greedy	21
Honeymoon Avenue	22
Wishful Thinking	24
Midnight Confession	25
Your Waiting Shed	26

Stolen Heart	27
Cruelest Dilemma	29
Silence	30
The Memory of Us	31
Love	32
Double-edged Sword	33
Psyche	34
Jade Evergreen	35
Rechelle	37
Immortalizing You	38
About the Author	*39*

Folklore

My love,
your very existence is a work of art.
Your beauty is a whole incantation
that has enchanted my foolish little heart.

If your body is a whole canvas,
then my lips will be the brushes.
I will make you my masterpiece
by painting colors all over your edges.

Now my tints are all over you
just like that night when we first met.
You recorded hymns and proverbs
on my buttons like a cassette.

And the fairytale of how we fell in love,
and how we watched sunsets on the shore,
will be passed down in the ages to come:
timeless and immortalized like folklore.

My Jennie

Love has never been this beautiful,
until I shared it with you.
It has never been this passionate
until you painted golden all of my blues.

They say that the eyes
are the windows of one's soul.
Is me being drawn to you,
just my heart answering to your call?

My love, if you only knew
how you occupy all of my waking days,
how you enchant all of me
with just your simple ways.

The echoes of your laughter:
they have become my favorite hymn.
An addicting tune, that fills me
with sunshine to the brim.

Now I sit beside you
just to simply watch you breathe.
How could you be so effortlessly beautiful?
Effortlessly irresistible?

My love,
we are a story that has to be told.
Your embrace is heaven's touch—
a daydream I am blessed to hold!

You Were

The clock marches on
just as the pages continuously turn,
our hands fit far perfectly
just for us to be each other's lesson learned.

As if the gaps between your fingers
are made to be filled with mine.
We almost had it —
we could have been divine.

The apple of my eye,
the subject of my dreams,
the center of my attention, and
the muse of my poems.

You were all of them at once.
You held that much power over me.
Who would have thought
that one day, I will be setting you free?

The Standard

I remember the day,
when you asked me for my standards.
I was left speechless —
I did not know what to answer.

I meticulously brainstormed
in hopes of listing down my reasons.
You have witnessed how I became silent —
I was questioning the need for qualifications.

Because I just woke up one day,
already caught up in this accidental chemistry.
Am I to be blamed,
for failing to explain the complexities of serendipity?

My love, how can I explain?
when my love for you
goes beyond the boundaries of reason.
I'm in love with everything that defines you.

I took a deep breath
and wrapped my arm in your shoulder.
In a serious tone — I uttered,
"My love, you are my standard."

You don't need to follow
a certain criteria for you
to be the subject of my affections.
I love you, because you're you.

One Last Time

One last time...
May I be greedy of your touch?
I will mark you with my scent;
am I asking for too much?

One last time...
May I be thirsty of your gaze?
Can I call you mine
like how it is back in the days?

One last time...
May you listen to my eyes?
With longings hidden deep within,
only you can recognize?

How much should I pay?
How long should I wait?
How far should I walk?
Just to be with you one last time?

Behold Her I

An alluvion of elegance,
an existence of perfection:
overflowing with charms,
sapience, and sophistication.

The twinkling of the stars
in the sparkle of her eyes,
enchants me everytime
like an addictive vice.

Behold her!
the epitome of beauty:
her that surpassed
even of Aphrodite's!

The way she moves,
her gestures are majesty.
Oh how privileged am I
to be her chosen devotee

Behold Her II

Her scent ambrosial
like the breath of spring.
Rivaling the dazzling sun
is her smile— radiating.

With her skin so soft,
gentle like a summer rain.
Her touch so addicting,
like the chemicals in my veins.

When I cannot help myself
but helplessly fall into your gravity
you are a breath of fresh air—
my euphoria and serendipity

The sound of your name—
how it tickles me to ecstasy.
Like how it is in fairytales,
will you runaway with me?

Your Eyes

Please,
don't take your eyes off of me.
You can't just charm all of my soul
and then tell it to break free.

Please,
don't take your eyes off of me.
Now I thirst for you gaze
where existing without you is cruelty.

Please,
don't take your eyes off of me.
Drown me with your scent,
in the vastness of this eternity.

Please,
don't take your eyes off of me.
Mark me with you kisses,
violet bruises— let it be.

Please,
don't take your eyes off of me.
I have grown far too fond of you
and it's driving me crazy— can't you see?

The Sweetest Con

They say, "forever is the sweetest con."
But darling, I beg to disagree.
It is your faithless love
by which I don't want to be set free.

It is my wishful thinking
of this hoax that I deeply believe in.
It is my blind devotion
of holding on unto this sweet nothing.

Oh, how sugar-sweet
it is to mindlessly dream!
Indeed, an ecstatic deception
where I'd end up crying a whole stream.

The world moves on,
the pages have been flipped.
Your "I love yous" are the sweetest con:
they still make my heart skip a beat.

Who Would Have Thought?

Who would have thought
that you'd enchant me just like this?
As if you're Aphrodite in disguise—
loving you was a utopian kiss!

Girl, if you only know
how you consume all of my waking days.
I am getting lost in the thoughts of you,
as if hypnotized by the magnet in your gaze.

You're a melody in my brain:
a tune indeed so addicting.
All these drugs can't compare,
from your touch that's intoxicating.

My euphoria, my lifeline—
you brought sunshine to my ghost town.
Happiness is vanity without you:
behold! a world drowned in an endless blue.

Serendipity

Meeting you was a twist of fate—
a magical stroke of serendipity.
As if the stars have finally collided;
as if tied by the red strings of destiny.

Meeting you was a kiss of heaven—
an enchanting touch of magic.
As if embraced by a gentle sunlight;
a feeling indeed ecstatic!

Loving you is a fairytale bliss—
an unexpected scheme of Cupid.
As if we're made for each other,
call me hopeless, call me stupid.

'Cause I'm losing my mind:
as if wrapped up in a beautiful accident.
And best things happen when it's unexpected—
so please, don't ever set me free from this entanglement

I Miss You

"I miss you."
I never knew how much
power these words hold
until it was spoken by you.

"I miss you."
You can utter this in my grave,
and watch, as it
breathe me back to life.

"I miss you."
Instead of butterflies in my stomach,
your words brought me
to the whole damn zoo.

Girl, I'm going crazy:
crazily addicted to you.
Telling me you miss me—
can you bear the consequence
of me, falling in love with you?

Questions

If this isn't love,

then why do my lips beam sunlight?

At the mere thought of your name—

as if telling me you're worth a fight?

If this isn't fate,

then why does this heart keep falling into motion?

Every time you are near,

I'm always on the edge of my emotions.

If you're not the one,

then why do you keep crossing the horizon of my mind?

Every day, every night–

you're sparing me no time to unwind.

Girl, you have bewitched all of me–

my body, my mind, and my soul.

I once thought my heart doesn't have room for love anymore;

but if it's you then I'd gladly fall.

Enslaved

How can I break free
when I am merely a slave to my emotions?
Both my hands are in shackles,
like a prisoner with no redemption.

How can I resist
when you are my greatest temptation?
The harder I try to overcome you,
the more I find myself in contradiction

Indeed! resistance is futile
I have no other choice but submission
this heartless love that tortures me
the snare that robbed me of my salvation

I watched myself fall from grace
as your touch became my new addiction.
Our late-night worship and your scarlet kiss:
they enslaved me like some intoxication.

Oh sweet and merciful heaven,
come and hear my plea!
If to long for her embrace is a felony
then indeed of this crime I am guilty!

With You

It's obvious clear as the day,
that I have grown fond of you.
I feel the heat of an Indian summer,
everytime you're in my view.

You came into my life
bearing sunshine in your smile:
now every second, every minute—
being in your company is worthwhile.

Long story short—
I've become a slave to my emotions.
Will you allow me to dream
of being the only subject of your affections?

I don't know if this is love,
you may call this infatuation;
but one thing is for certain:
I'm most happy when I'm with this person.

Superman

His sight reached
unto a fair maiden in trouble.
With terror painted on her face—
agitated by this tiny scroll.

Scrolls that hold inscriptions
as to whom to be burned at the stake.
She picked one from the goblet,
and alas! she got it by mistake.

As if played by fate,
luck just wasn't on her favor.
In this losing game,
who will be her saviour?

With a voice like thunder
he mightily shouted,
"Have no fear,
for I, Superman is here."

Greedy

Just this once,
will you allow me to be greedy?
Greedy of your touch—
truly, madly, deeply?

The depths of the ocean:
that's what I saw in your eyes.
Can you blame me if I longed
to sink deeper into you— free of price?

Together with this magic
I feel sparks coming into view.
Will you grant me this honor—
the honor of loving you?

I yearn to hold you:
to feel the warmth of your breath;
to spoil you with my kisses;
to crown you with laurel wreath.

Honeymoon Avenue

The night was at its peak,
when I leaned towards your ear:
whispering my admirations,
and how much I hold you dear.

Crystal-clear in my mind,
was your skin of fragrant posies
as we drown at each other's gaze;
while on a bed of blood-red roses.

I stared at your charcoal-dark eyes,
as they seemed to crave my touch.
It was affirmed when you kissed me
I was fuel: your body was the match.

Roaming briskly like wildfire
were your fingers in my buttons.
I got ready to pull the trigger
as my Levi's fell in sequence.

I felt a surge of my emotions,
like a wave the ocean just can't control.
I once thought we do not click;
but now you're playing with my rifle.

Wishful Thinking

When the time comes,
when my pen runs out of ink:
when my mind becomes void of magic
no matter how hard I think.

When the time comes,
when this love runs out of warmth;
with sparks fading,
and thrills evaporating.

When the time comes,
when I would reek of imperfection:
my flaws magnified,
as I stare at my broken reflection.

When the time comes
when my tongue fails to even utter my name:
may you look into my eyes
and still love me the same.

Midnight Confession

The deeper the night goes,
the longer I think of you
in this sleepless solitude
where longings come into view.

As I count the falling raindrops;
my thoughts echo your name.
I should've learned how to gamble—
to better play my cards in this love game.

Here comes the inevitable:
the very truth unvarnished.
Wishing every moment froze—
those times that had me astonished.

Along the time's never ceasing march,
here's me reflecting relentlessly:
seasons change, others moved on
yet I'm still here where you left me.

Your Waiting Shed

And I soon came to realize:
this is the farthest that we'll ever go.
You seemed happy without me
hence, I'm bidding you my adieu.

Vanity are my gloves
when I was never been your match,
but how do I untangle
these strings that in the first place, weren't even attached?

While I am just a line in your story,
you are a whole poetry to me.
But this was never a story of us—
I was foolish to believe it might be.

Perhaps, I was just your waiting shed—
your shelter on a passing storm.
What fight do I have
in comparison to him: your home?

Stolen Heart

It was the dead of the night
when she broke down my defenses.
I never felt a thing,
as if she numbed all of my senses.

Like a heat of a New York minute,
it eventuate in a swift—
my heart has gone missing
but who really is the thief?

And then I found you in the balcony
enjoying cigarettes like a villain
with my heart in your palm
and a grinning face— you're chillin'

But nowhere to be heard
are the sirens of police cars.
are the cops her accomplice?
it appears as if they are.

"Can you give it back to me?"
I pleaded like a beggar.
She then rolled your eyes
and declared that it's hers forever.

Cruelest Dilemma

The cruelest dilemma I've ever known
is the conflict between the mind and heart.
It is losing all of my rationality,
I can't seem to make decisions right.

Stuck & between these extremes,
am I perhaps being toyed by fate?
To lose all my sense of reason:
this perfectly sounds like my current state.

When the dusk falls,
I am a slave to my emotions.
But with the arrival of dawn,
I am a master of my reasons.

I would tell you, "I miss you"
as dictated by my heart,
only for my mind to intervene
saying, "That's no longer your part."

Silence

Your absence speaks volumes
in the form of this solitude.
It is the feeling of being lost
amidst an assembled multitude.

We were once tied up with calls,
now you're cutting off our telephone wires.
I wrote you letters
just for you to address them to the fire.

You reached for your phone
and played silence on speakers:
it was bursting loud,
it was shaking the whole ground.

With storms on my eyes
and the rain blurring my vision;
I stare absentmindedly at my sole witness —
my tears-soaked cushion.

The Memory of Us

How I longed for those days
when the world was our oyster,
the pavement was our runway
on shades of gold and silver.

Chasing butterflies on green meadows:
we were the paragon of romance
back when we lived in a teenage dream
where I lose myself in your glance.

Now I'm left
with these promises that we made.
covered in doubts—
if should I fight or just let them fade.

All these memories with you
that once brought me to heaven
now is torture in my mind:
should've banished them to oblivion.

Love

I'm currently paced to my 20th
but when will I truly learn?
that love isn't just an emotion
neither just a simple yearn.

It is not about the cards
nor it is the alignment of the stars
but the language of lost souls
where I paint colors at your scars.

It's not about the sparks,
but the rainbow after the storm.
Love is staring at your eyes
and seeing the warmth of a home.

Love is commitment,
not just a simple trend—
it is dancing in the pouring rain
and watching destiny bend.

Double-edged Sword

A sword double-edged
is this love so treacherous!
Just like playing with fire,
it was a feeling indeed disastrous.

I warned myself with the sparks:
they're paralleled with burns.
For a second we'll have ecstasy,
then followed by agony; they take turns

A sword double-edged,
but why do I still dream of you?
In these cold nights of December
I reflect in search for a clue.

All in blur: my eyes were hazy,
like a drug it drives me crazy.
With all these knowledge that I have,
why do I still long for this love?

Psyche

My love,
Pysche is thy name.
You have transcended even Aphrodite
in beauty and in fame.

You are a well of elegance—
a fountain that doesn't run dry;
in the changes of season,
in the passage of time.

Like the stars in the night sky,
I exist to only shine for you.
like a candle in the wind,
I will gladly melt too.

I am the god Eros
and I command love with my own bow.
Who would have known
that I too shall fall victim of my own arrow?

Jade Evergreen

There she goes:
the center of my sight.
Just as dreams are meant to be chased,
In pursuit of you— I ran with all my might.

Fueled by this adoration,
I poured all of me navigating our future:
our kids, our home —
I was trying to paint the whole picture.

I never thought anything could go wrong
as everything unfolded with perfection.
I was blinded by your reassurance,
I mistook it with reciprocation.

You secured me with you words,
you warmed me with your embraces,
just for you to text me one night
that there was never an I in your future.

Perhaps, loving you
is me being deprived of chances,
and to hold on
is me balancing on breaking branches.

Rechelle

Roses die of shame as they no longer
Enchant me quite as you do.
Call me a sucker, call me a pushover:
Helpless are my reasons if we're together.
Everything of me is hypnotized, shackled
Like an old fashioned slave.
Let me go not, don't ever set me free.
Eternally yours: this I dream to be.

Immortalizing You

In all these poems
your essence I entwine.
Our memories I engrave
like a timeless ode— divine.

In words I paint your beauty
through stanzas I emblazon your grace
through this eternal ink,
I freeze the warmth of your embrace.

In this garden of metaphors,
your laughter shall echo timelessly.
In every verse,
they shall scream your name unceasingly.

In this dance of rhymes
I etch our tale with my heart imbued.
Behold! the testament of my love:
to immortalize you.

About the Author

Marcel T. Despabeladero

Marcel T. Despabeladero, 22, is an emerging writer and a Bachelor of Secondary Education major in English student at Negros Oriental State University – Guihulngan City Campus. Passionate about language and storytelling, he has actively engaged in student leadership, serving as Vice President of the Drama, Debate, and English Society (DDES) in 2023–2024, where he led initiatives to enhance students' communication and creativity. A member of the League of Student Organizations, he supports campus-wide student engagement. Marcel is a grateful recipient of multiple educational grants, including the CHED Tertiary Education Subsidy and support from various government offices. These opportunities fuel his literary pursuits, which often center on love, longing, heartbreak, and memory. His debut poetry collection, Writings of a Random Bachelor, reflects his lyrical style and belief in the power of words to capture emotion and preserve fleeting moments. Marcel continues to grow as a writer, committed to both education and creative expression.

www.ingramcontent.com/pod-product-compliance
Lightning Source LLC
LaVergne TN
LVHW041558070526
838199LV00046B/2042